DINO-MIKE

AND THE
LUNAR SHOWDOWN

WRITTEN & ILLUSTRATED BY FRANCO

STONE ARCH BOOKS

a capstone imprint

Dino-Mike! is published by
Stone Arch Books,
a Capstone imprint
1710 Roe Crest Drive
North Mankato, Minnesota 56003
www.mycapstone.com

Cataloging-in-Publication Data is available on
the Library of Congress website.

ISBN: 978-1-4965-2492-8 (library hardcover)
ISBN: 978-1-4965-2496-6 (paperback)
ISBN: 978-1-4965-2500-0 (eBook)

Summary: Having been defeated in Australia and
Antarctica, Mr. Bones hides out somewhere he's
sure he won't be found: the Moon!

Printed in Canada.
009635F16

CONTENTS

Young Mike Evans travels the world with his dino-hunting dad and his best friend, Shannon. From the Jurassic Coast in Great Britain to the Liaoning Province in China, young Dino-Mike has been there, *dug* that!

When his dad is dusting fossils, Mike's boning up on his own dino skills — only he's finding the real deal. A live T. rex egg! A portal to the Jurassic Period!! An undersea dinosaur sanctuary!!!

Prepare yourself for another wild and wacky Dino-Mike adventure, which nobody will ever believe . . .

Chapter 1
MOON LANDING

"This is awesome!" shouted
Dino-Mike as his feet hit the ground. He
jumped again, soaring twenty feet into
the air. "Whoa!" he screamed excitedly.

"You act like this is your first time on
the Moon," said his friend Shannon.

Dino-Mike landed next to her on
the powdery lunar surface. "This *is* my
first time on the Moon," Mike told her,
looking puzzled. "What — you've been
here before?"

"My dad took us here a couple of times," replied Shannon. She looked over at her brother — and Mike's former archenemy — Jurassic Jeff.

Jeff nodded. "Yeah," he confirmed. "But we weren't here for very long."

"How could you not mention something like that?" Mike exclaimed.

"It didn't seem like a big deal," Shannon said, plainly.

Mike couldn't believe his ears. "Visiting the Moon isn't a big deal?!" he shouted.

"I barely remember it," added Shannon. "We came when our dad was first testing the teleportation portal. We didn't have these fancy suits or anything." She tugged her ultrathin exosuit, which her dad had recently invented.

Shannon's father had also invented Mike's Dino Jacket. The high-tech hoodie was equipped with dozens and dozens of gadgets, which had saved Dino-Mike's life on more than one adventure.

In fact, the jacket was saving his life right now, he thought. Before landing on the Moon, he'd switched his hoodie into Space Mode 2.0. This newly designed feature allowed Mike to breathe and protected him from the harsh environment of outer space.

"The first time we came to the Moon," Shannon continued, "we came in a clear, Plexiglas box — kind of like a fish tank. We couldn't move around."

"Ugh!" exclaimed Jurassic Jeff, remembering the trip. "It was soOOooOOo boring!" he said. "We were stuck in that box for, like, five hours with nothing to do and nowhere to go."

"But you were still on the MOON!" Dino-Mike repeated.

Shannon and Jurassic Jeff both shrugged.

"Okay, okay, the Moon is pretty cool," Jeff finally admitted. "But we still have a job to do, remember?"

Dino-Mike went over the past week in his head. Only days ago, they'd been in Antarctica, tracking Li Jing Jiang and Chiang Jiang.

Or, as Jurassic Jeff liked to call them, the Bones Twins (even though they were only siblings — not twins). The Boneses were using their father's technology to bring dinosaur fossils back to life. But when things got hairy, they teleported the dinosaurs to a secret location.

Dino-Mike and his friends believed that they'd finally found the Boneses' hiding spot!

"Come on," added Jeff, turning and walking away. "We have to get going. The Earth will be setting soon."

Jurassic Jeff headed toward a deep shadow on the horizon: the dark side of the Moon.

Chapter 2

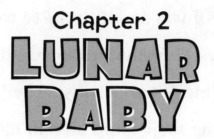

"Do you know that the same side of the Moon always faces Earth?" said Dino-Mike, repeating a question his father had asked him once.

Shannon and Jurassic Jeff stopped walking and turned to face Mike. "Of course we know that!" they both said together.

"Why do you think we're headed there?" added Shannon.

Dino-Mike thought for a second.

Duh! If you needed to hide a few dinosaurs, the Moon was perfect. But the far side of the Moon was an even better hiding spot. No one on Earth would ever see them — even with a superpowered telescope!

As Mike stepped across the Moon's shadowy boundary, he looked up. There were so many stars, and he could see them so clearly. He nearly tripped because he was looking up instead of where he was walking.

When he did look down, Dino-Mike noticed his footprints in the soil.

"Cool!" he exclaimed. "My footprints are on the Moon!"

"Come on!" Jeff scolded. "You'll never find dinosaurs in the dirt."

Just then, Dino-Mike noticed small triangle marks all over the surface. *That's weird.* He bent down to take a closer look.

The shapes weren't triangle marks, after all. They were claw marks!

"What are you looking at?" asked Shannon.

"I found these marks on the ground," answered Mike. "They shouldn't be out here, right?

Both Jeff and Shannon were bent down looking at them.

They knew the Bones Twins were transporting dinosaurs to the Moon, but how were they keeping them alive? Dinosaurs needed air to breathe just like any other living creature.

How could they be walking around on the Moon?

"Those are little T. rex claws!" Jurassic Jeff finally said. "Spread out and see if you can find where they lead."

After about a minute of searching, Shannon stopped and stared at one particular spot on the ground. "Um, guys?" she began.

As Mike moved closer, he saw what Shannon was staring at. "That's just one of our boot prints," he told her.

"Yeah, I know," Shannon shot back, "but why is that baby T. rex claw mark on top of the boot print?"

Dino-Mike's eyes grew wide. He looked over at Jurassic Jeff and then back to Shannon.

ROOOAAAAR! A familiar sound rumbled behind them. They all spun slowly around.

"Over there!" shouted Shannon, pointing toward a nearby crater.

A small dinosaur stepped out of the crater and stomped toward them.

"Uh-oh." Mike gulped.

Chapter 3
SPACE SUITS FOR DINOS

"Wait — what am I looking at?"
Dino-Mike asked, staring at the dinosaur
charging toward them. "Is that a —?"

"Baby T. rex!" Jurassic Jeff finished
his thought.

"In a space suit?" Shannon added,
puzzled.

The baby T. rex was indeed dressed
in a space suit!

As the beast continued toward them,
it snarled and roared, fogging up the
fishbowl helmet on its head.

The tyrannosaurus darted past them and then back around, in an almost playful manner. Dino-Mike remembered his last encounter with a baby T. rex. If he'd learned one thing about them, it was that baby dinosaurs acted like, well, babies!

Shannon bent down to pick up the tiny dino but pulled back when the T. rex snapped its jaws at her. Shannon laughed when she realized that the dinosaur couldn't really do any harm to her while wearing the helmet.

"He's a feisty one!" said Shannon as she reached for the dino again and picked it up.

"Where did he come from?" asked Jurassic Jeff, looking around at the barren landscape. "And why is he dressed up like that?"

"It's obvious," Shannon asserted. She inspected the space suit on the dinosaur more closely. "The Boneses have been transporting dinosaurs of all shapes and sizes up here. After a while, they probably ran out of room to keep them inside."

"So the Boneses are building space suits for them?" Jeff asked.

"Makes sense," said Mike. "How else would you store so many dinosaurs in a place that had no air?"

"What a horrible idea!" Jurassic Jeff shouted. "What if this suit didn't work? What kind of cruel, horrible people are they?!"

"That's why they're called the bad guys," Mike explained.

"Thanks," said Shannon, rolling her eyes. "I hadn't figured that one out."

Suddenly, Dino-Mike noticed that his shadow was getting longer on the ground. He watched as the blackness spread over the rocky surface of the Moon. At first, Mike wondered if the sun was setting really, really fast.

That can't be right, he thought.

Dino-Mike looked up. Something was blocking out the sun entirely . . .

"Mama T. rex!" Mike cried to get the attention of Jeff and Shannon.

Shannon and Jurassic Jeff turned.

A giant, usually very quick T. rex was slowly lumbering toward them. The Moon's low gravity made it difficult for the dinosaur to walk — not to mention that the T. rex was wearing a monster-sized space suit.

"HAHAHA!" Dino-Mike couldn't help but laugh.

"Do you think this is funny?" asked Jurassic Jeff.

"No, but —" Mike stopped and then let out another laugh. "Okay, yeah, it is kind of funny."

"Do you believe this?" said Jeff, turning to Shannon. "He thinks this is funny."

Shannon snickered. "You have to admit, Jeff, it's a little funny."

They all watched the T. rex bound up and down as it tried to reach them.

"You guys have no respect for the creatures of the Earth!" Jeff yelled.

"We're not on Earth," said Shannon, gesturing to the dinosaur. "That's why this is so funny."

Mike looked at the restless baby T. rex in Shannon's arms. "Why is that little guy able to run around so quickly compared to its momma?" he wondered aloud.

Shannon looked down at the baby T. rex. "Hmm," she said, thinking. "You're right. This little guy was zipping all over the place, but Momma looks like she's in slow motion."

"Maybe the baby T. rex is used to being out here, and she isn't," suggested Jurassic Jeff.

Dino-Mike's eyes widened. "You think that the Bones Twins are teaching their dinosaurs to moonwalk?" he said, thinking it was a silly question.

"Exactly!" exclaimed Jeff.

"Let's follow the mother T. rex," Shannon suggested. "I have a feeling that there are more dinosaurs wherever she came from."

Shannon placed the baby T. rex onto the ground. The little dinosaur darted back in the direction from which it had come. The giant momma dinosaur followed after, as quickly as she could.

"What are we waiting for?" Jurassic Jeff asked. "Let's jet!"

Jeff leaped into the air and ignited a high-tech rocket pack on his back.

FWOOOOOSH!

Jeff soared up, up, up — high above the Moon's surface.

FWOOOOOSH! FWOOOOOSH!

Dino-Mike and Shannon did the same, igniting their own packs and joining him high above the surface.

Shannon and Jeff's father, Dr. Broome, had invented the rocket packs. The packs didn't run on normal fuel. Instead, each pack released pressurized air, pushing them off the ground like deflating balloons.

Dino-Mike's eyes followed the baby T. rex and mother as they headed toward the horizon. A large structure peeked over a crater near them.

"Look!" shouted Mike, pointing toward the structure. "I see something up ahead."

"I see it, too," Shannon agreed. "It looks like some kind of warehouse."

"We should walk from here," said Jurassic Jeff, not wanting the Boneses to spot them.

Each of them decreased the air pressure on their packs, and they slowly descended back toward the Moon's powdery surface.

"What do you think the Boneses have planned?" Dino-Mike asked as they started toward the structure on foot.

"No idea," Jeff replied. "But the one thing I do know is that the Boneses are both completely crazy."

"Let's just hope all of their dinosaurs are as slow as that momma T. rex," Shannon added.

ROOOAAAAR!

Dino-Mike turned at the terrible sound. "I think we're about to find out!" he screamed.

Chapter 4
MOONQUAKE

"Is that an —?" Jeff began, staring at another giant dinosaur.

"Allosaurus!" Shannon shouted.

"Where did it come from?" asked Dino-Mike.

"Never mind that! Why isn't it wearing a space suit?" Jeff said.

The beast opened its jaws again, letting out a deafening roar through its razor-sharp teeth.

Then the allosaurus charged!

Unlike the T. rex, this dinosaur moved at full-speed. It ran at them like an out-of-control school bus.

"Keep him busy!" Jurassic Jeff commanded. He removed his backpack and began searching through it. "I'll set a trap."

Shannon waved her arms at the allosaurus. "Over here!" she shouted at the giant beast. The allosaurus immediately turned toward Shannon with its snapping jaws.

"Shannon!" screamed Dino-Mike. Then he looked over at Jurassic Jeff. "Jeff, a little help?"

"I'm still looking for the trap!" Jeff continued digging through his pack. "I know it's in here somewhere!"

"Try something else! Anything!" Shannon pleaded as the allosaurus chased her around and around a nearby crater.

Then suddenly, she tripped! The allosaurus was directly above her.

Shannon rolled onto her back and
got a worm's-eye view of the allosaurus's
monstrous jaws. "Help!" she screamed.

Dino-Mike knew he wasn't going to
get there in time. He felt completely
helpless. He could only watch as the
dinosaur moved in and then . . . stopped.

"Why did it stop?" Mike started to ask but got his answer when the ground started to tremble.

RUMMMMMMMMBBBBLLLLEE

"What is that?" asked Shannon as she clutched the ground. The allosaurus was doing the same thing, digging its giant claws into the Moon's powdery surface.

Mike dropped to his hands and knees as the ground shook. The dinosaur had stopped its attack momentarily and that gave him time to help Shannon.

He prepared to charge at the dino when he spotted Jeff holding a small black box. Jeff was winding up like a baseball pitcher and threw the box.

As the box landed, the high-tech device opened and a giant blue cube erected around the dinosaur. He was frozen in his spot, unable to move!

"Trap-o-saurus!" Mike exclaimed. He remembered the electronic dinosaur traps from previous expeditions, but he didn't know Jeff had brought any along.

With the allosaurus caged, Shannon stood and strode toward Jurassic Jeff. "You said that you weren't going to bring those things!" she shouted, madly.

"What are you talking about, Shannon?" Dino-Mike said, stepping between the siblings. "Jeff just saved your life with that trap-o-saurus."

"I'm not talking about the trap-o-saurus," Shannon replied, her gaze not leaving Jeff's eyes. "I'm talking about the seismic pellets."

"Huh?" Mike asked, puzzled.

"Take it easy, Shannon," Jeff told his sister. "I did bring the pellets, but I didn't used them. I swear!"

"Then how else do you explain what just happened?" asked Shannon.

Jurassic Jeff shrugged. "I don't know. But I didn't cause the quake."

"Wait — what's a seismic pellet?" Mike interrupted.

"It's a device that causes a localized, Richter-level event," Shannon explained.

"Huh?" Mike said again.

"It's how Jeff caused the earthquake that made the dinosaur stop in its tracks," she added. "They're dangerous and unpredictable, and both my dad and I told him not to use them or bring them!"

"Believe it or not, Shannon," said Jurassic Jeff, "I didn't cause the quake."

"If you're talking about the moonquake," Mike began, "I read those things happen pretty often up here."

"Huh?" Shannon asked this time.

"Yeah," Mike confirmed. "Moonquakes happen all the time up here, but they're not as severe as on Earth because of the low gravity here."

"See!" Jeff exclaimed, smiling boastfully. "I told you I didn't use it!"

"You still brought them!" Shannon accused him.

"Well, yeah . . . " Jeff's smile disappeared.

Mike knew Shannon well enough to know that if she thought something wasn't a good idea it probably wasn't.

"I was only going to use them if we got in real trouble," Jeff explained.

KA-BOOOOM!! The ground suddenly exploded beneath their feet!

Dino-Mike flew above the surface, floated back to the ground, and landed with a silent **THUD**. "Ugh!" he said, standing and dusting off his Dino Jacket.

When he finally looked up, Mike spotted the long, spiky tail of an ankylosaurus swinging at him.

FWOOOOOSH! Mike ducked just in time, and the razor-sharp spikes whizzed inches from his face. This dinosaur wasn't wearing a space suit either.

How can he breathe without oxygen? Mike wondered as he ducked again.

After a moment, the ankylosaurus turned its attention to Shannon and Jeff. The siblings had gotten to their feet and were on the move. The ankylosaurus swung its tail around and — **SMASH!** — narrowly missed them again. Mike knew they couldn't dodge the tail much longer.

Dino-Mike leaped into action!

He ran up behind the ankylosaurus and grabbed hold of its spiky tail. Then he pressed a button on his Dino Jacket.

FWIP! FWIP! Two giant mechanical claws burst from his sleeves. As they latched onto the dinosaur's tail, Mike pressed another button.

FWOOOOOSH! His rocket pack ignited, and Dino-Mike flew into the sky — along with the ankylosaurus!

"Woohoo!" Shannon and Jeff shouted up at him.

Dino-Mike flew through the air with the dinosaur, but soon his mechanical claws began to creak and crack.

Mike knew that the claws couldn't handle the weight of the dino much longer. He released the claws, and the ankylosaurus smashed back onto the lunar surface with a **THUD**.

Mike rocketed toward his friends.

"Mike, that was insane!" Jeff exclaimed as he returned.

"He's going to try and attack again," Mike warned. "Any more of those dino traps?"

"Just one," Jeff replied.

In the distance, the ankylosaurus rose to its feet. It lurched forward and then something weird happened. They could see its eyes turn red.

Dino-Mike gulped. "Well, we better make it count."

Chapter 5
RED EYES

Jurassic Jeff quickly pulled the trap-o-saurus from his backpack. He held his finger over the On switch as the ankylosaurus charged toward the trio.

"Three . . ." Mike began to count.

"Two . . ." Shannon continued as the dinosaur's red eyes grew closer.

"One . . . !" Jurassic Jeff shouted, preparing to flip on the electric trap.

Suddenly, the dinosaur stopped and looked around, locating a distant sound.

Then the ankylosaurus turned and started walking away from them.

"Where's it going?" Dino-Mike followed it, but not too closely.

"Whoa!" said Shannon. "Look at the allosaurus."

They all turned to look at the dinosaur encased in the bright, electric trap. Its eyes were also glowing red.

Dino-Mike studied the ankylosaurus marching steadily away from them. "If we let the allosaurus out of the containment field, do you think it would follow the ankylosaurus?" he wondered.

Shannon already knew what Mike was thinking.

"Do you think the red eyes mean that they're under some sort of control?" she asked him.

"Remote-controlled robots?!" Jeff exclaimed. "You two are crazy!"

"Look around, Jeff," Dino-Mike said, pointing out at the lunar landscape. "We're standing on the surface of the Moon being chased by dinosaurs that haven't existed in millions of years. This whole thing is crazy, don't you think?"

"Good point," Jeff conceded. "Well, just get ready to act if this allosaurus does anything but walk away." Then he bent down to turn off the electric trap.

As soon as the blue cube field came down, the allosaurus turned and followed the other dinosaur — just as Dino-Mike had predicted.

"They're probably being called to home base," Shannon guessed.

"Then we'll follow them," said Jeff, "and take down Mr. Bones!"

Dino-Mike was excited, but a little scared at the same time. After a moment, he picked up his pack and followed the dinosaurs as they trudged slowly away.

About forty-five minutes of walking later, Mike could see other dinosaurs gathering into an area up ahead. "That must be where Mr. Bones is hiding," Mike said, pointing at the large warehouse in the distance.

"Right," said Jeff. "Fan out. We need to get an equal distance apart around the perimeter and set up the stakes."

Jeff removed a dozen metal rods from his backpack and distributed them equally. The rods looked like simple tent stakes, but they were much more. Created by Dr. Broome, these high-tech devices worked like superpowered lightning rods. The stakes could be planted around a large area and act like a makeshift electric fence.

"Once the stakes are set up," Shannon said, "we sync them to the power battery and then everything inside becomes trapped."

"Got it," Dino-Mike confirmed.

Shannon grabbed his arm. "Be careful," she said.

"She's right," said Jeff. "Get as close as you can, but whatever you do, don't get spotted." Then he walked straight toward the warehouse, waving as he left.

Shannon headed to the left, and Dino-Mike finally headed to the right.

After walking a good distance, Dino-Mike heard Jeff's voice come over the radio. "I'm in position," he said.

"Me too," came Shannon's voice soon after.

Mike moved toward Mr. Bones's base until he could almost see inside. He didn't dare get any closer just in case.

"I'm in position," he finally confirmed.

Jeff's voice crackled over the radio again. "Okay, plant your stakes and wait for my signal to activate."

Mike set out the equipment and began to dig a hole for the first stake.

Mike put one end of the rod into the hole and began to push soil around it. All he had to do now was wait for Jurassic Jeff to hook up the battery power and sync the other rods to it. Once they did that, the base — and everything inside — would be trapped in a fence of electricity.

Just then, Dino-Mike thought he heard something come through his radio. *Was that Jeff's signal?* he wondered. Then another crack came through his headset.

"Hey, guys, did you hear that?" Dino-Mike radioed his friends.

"What was that?" Shannon replied.

"I don't know," Dino-Mike said. "Jeff, do you know?"

Silence.

"Jeff?" Mike asked again.

Still no response.

"Do you think something happened to his microphone?" Mike asked Shannon.

She didn't respond this time either.

"Shannon?" he asked after a few seconds, but all he heard was silence.

Something must have happened.

Suddenly, Dino-Mike felt the ground rumble again. *Maybe Jurassic Jeff finally used those seismic pellets he was talking about,* Mike thought.

But then he could see an underground line being formed in the soil. A second later — **SPOOOSH!** — an Oryctodromeus cubicularis burst out of the lunar surface.

This car-size dino seemed to be functioning without a space suit. The other thing Mike noticed right away is that it didn't have glowing red eyes. This dinosaur was either moving under its own actions or it was being controlled manually.

The dinosaur, not finding its prey, grabbed the electric stake with its jaw. It ripped the metal rod apart as if it were made of cardboard. Then the creature turned and quickly buried itself back underground.

The stake was destroyed.

Jeff and Shannon were not answering Mike's calls.

Dino-Mike had a bad feeling about the whole plan, but he felt odd in a different way too. Mike felt like he was being watched.

He turned around to find a towering figured dressed in all black standing behind him . . .

"Mr. Bones," Dino-Mike grumbled.

Chapter 6
SURRENDER

"Are my friends all right?" Mike asked Mr. Bones.

Mr. Bones stood silent.

"Answer me!!" Dino-Mike screamed. But then Mike remembered that he was wearing a soundproof helmet.

Oops!

Mr. Bones remained silent and pointed toward his base. Mike understood that Mr. Bones wanted him to go there.

As they walked in that direction, Mike could feel the glowing red eyes of dinosaurs following them.

When they neared the entrance of the base, Mike noticed dinosaurs lined up on both sides of the entrance. They looked like security guards armed with deadly teeth. Mike eyed them nervously as he walked past and into the open doors of the compound.

Once inside, Dino-Mike heard a muffled voice. Mike realized that it was Mr. Bones speaking to him.

"You can take off your . . . helmet?" said the voice. "We're in a pressurized atmosphere. There's air here."

Dino-Mike pressed a button on the hood of his Dino Jacket.

BEEP!

The Plexiglas shield slid apart and into the sides of the hoodie. He took a deep breath before sliding the hoodie off of his head too.

Dino-Mike noticed Mr. Bones looking on, impressed. Ever since their first encounter, Mr. Bones had wanted Mike's high-tech hoodie for himself.

"What did you do with my friends?" Mike immediately asked.

"They haven't been harmed," Mr. Bones replied. "But they will be soon . . . and so will you."

Dino-Mike looked around to see if he could spot Jeff and Shannon anywhere. The place looked like a giant toy store. There were dinosaurs of every kind everywhere in the room. Most were in cages, so they couldn't get out. Some had glowing eyes while others wore various space suits.

At first glance, Dino-Mike thought Mr. Bones's technology had to be improving — or worsening, depending on how you looked at it.

"What's with all the dinosaurs with different space suits?" Mike asked.

"I'm sure you're wondering about the ones without space suits even more," replied Mr. Bones.

"Now that you mention it . . ." Mike started.

"It's difficult to put a space suit on a dinosaur," Mr. Bones said, chuckling. "I should know. I've put them on quite a few dinosaurs." He started to walk around the compound. "I mean, we . . ."

Mr. Bones paused.

Dino-Mike knew Mr. Bones was thinking about his sister Li Jing. Mike and his friends had captured Li Jing on their last expedition to Antarctica.

"We," Mr. Bones continued, "were bringing lots of dinosaurs up here. We realized very quickly that we were running out of room. If we wanted to keep going with our plan, we needed to find a way feed them and house them. Then we came up with the idea that there was a whole Moon out there that they could run around on."

Mr. Bones pointed to a dinosaur wearing a space suit.

"However," he continued, "our first space suits weren't strong enough for the Moon's harsh environment."

Mr. Bones moved in front of a dinosaur without a space suit. "But then," he said, "We met you . . . Dino-Mike. When we first tangled in China, I got my first glimpse of your amazing Dino Jacket. I knew we had to have it. I knew it was the key to making things work for us here on the Moon."

"What do you mean?" Dino-Mike asked. He didn't understand.

How does my Dino Jacket have anything to do with these space suits, he wondered.

"I wasn't able to get your jacket," Mr. Bones explained. "But I did manage to gather a green fiber from it." In his palm was a tiny green thread, which shimmered like Mike's Dino Jacket.

"Huh?" Mike asked, still puzzled.

"We analyzed that thread and discovered the wondrous material it was made out of," said Mr. Bones. "Nothing we've ever seen before! And with that material, we developed the . . . invisible space suit!"

Dino-Mike couldn't believe what he was hearing — and not seeing!

"I can tell by the look on your face that you're surprised!" said Mr. Bones.

"But you haven't even heard the best part," Mr. Bones said. "The material is the lightest and most breathable material in the universe — perfect for space. We were able to infuse the suits with oxygen, so there's no need for bulky tanks."

Dino-Mike stared at him in disbelief.

Mr. Bones's skull face got close to Mike. "You don't get it do you?" he asked. "Your Dino Jacket made all of this possible, Dino-Mike!"

Dino-Mike's eyes widened. He couldn't believe what he was hearing. Mr. Bones had now found a way to get to all the technology and dinosaurs he ever wanted because of him.

"Now it's time for you to hand over that Dino Jacket!" demanded Mr. Bones.

"Why?" Mike asked. "You have the technology. You don't need it anymore."

"No," Mr. Bones agreed, "but you do! Without it, you'll never defeat my sister or me again. And you'll never leave here!"

Dino-Mike felt defeated. He knew that he had no choice but to give up the high-tech hoodie. He just needed one thing first.

"Before I give you the jacket," he told Mr. Bones, "I want to see that my friends are okay."

"No!" Mr. Bones responded. "You have no choice here. I'm not falling for tricks." He held out his hand. "The jacket. Now."

Dino-Mike started to unzip his jacket. As he did, he looked around for any sign of his friends. All he saw were dinosaurs in various space suits and ones with invisible suits.

Wait a minute, he suddenly thought, *maybe my Dino Jacket can become invisible too!*

He'd never considered the possibility before. Why would he have? But now, that possibility seemed like the only way out.

Mike zipped his jacket back up. "Wait a second," he started. "How do I know my friends are really okay?"

"You don't," said Mr. Bones. "Now stop stalling!" He stepped closer to Mike with an outstretched hand. "Give me the jacket. Right now!"

"What happens if it's not here?" asked Mike.

"What?" asked Mr. Bones. "Don't play any games with me, kid. I don't have time for it."

"It's not a game," said Dino-Mike. He smiled and then . . . disappeared.

Chapter 7
NOW YOU SEE ME . . .

Dino-Mike had remembered Dr. Broome telling him about a secret combination of buttons on his Dino Jacket. He'd said, "If you press them in the right order, you'll experience something you've never seen."

Hitting those buttons turned the exterior of his jacket into a cloaking device. Dino-Mike was invisible! He couldn't help but chuckle.

It really was something he's never seen! Mike thought.

"Where are you, Dino-Mike?!" shouted Mr. Bones, standing just inches from him. "I can hear you laughing!"

Dino-Mike moved quickly away. He frantically searched the base for Jeff and Shannon. After a moment, Mike could see Mr. Bones making wild hand gestures in the air. He knew Mr. Bones was controlling the dinosaurs to attack.

Uh-oh! Dino-Mike thought.

Even though he was invisible, Dino-Mike knew that plenty of dinosaurs could sniff him out.

FLAP! FLAP! FLAP! Just then, Dino-Mike heard a familiar flapping sound above his head. He'd heard the sound before.

But where? he wondered.

Suddenly Mike realized where he'd heard the sound before. He quickly ducked. And just in time!

FWOOOOOOSH!

"C. Yangi!" Mike cried. The turkey-like dinosaur swooped past his head. The dino's sharp claw ripped a small piece from his Dino Jacket.

The C. Yangi flew over and around him, coming in for another pass. Mike ran for cover. He crashed into a nearby desk and knocked over a file cabinet.

SMASH!

Mr. Bones turned toward the commotion and then signaled the dinosaur into that direction.

The C. Yangi dove toward Dino-Mike like a furious hawk. He had nowhere to hide! Nowhere to run!

At the last moment, Dino-Mike squeezed the zipper on his invisible Dino Jacket. **FWOOOOOSH!** The high-tech hoodie blew up like a balloon.

At the same time, the C. Yangi struck Dino-Mike. **BOING!!** The deadly bird bounced off the Dino Jacket like a rubber ball off a brick wall.

"NOoooOOOooO!" Mr. Bones screamed through his teeth. Then he thrust his hands into the air, and the ground started to shake.

Burrowing dinosaurs! Dino-Mike thought.

An alarm sounded in Mike's ear. *The heat sensors!* he remembered.

The invisible space suits must have a heat source! I can track them!

Dino-Mike tracked the underground dinosaur and waited for it to surface.

CRAAAAASH! An oryctodromeus burst through the floor, but Mike was ready. He pressed a button and three stegosaurus-like plates popped out of his Dino Jacket.

Blue electric energy shot out of the plates, striking the burrowing dino. The oryctodromeus quickly froze in place.

"Yes!" Dino-Mike shouted in celebration, but then he quickly covered his mouth.

Too late! Mr. Bones's next dinosaur was already stomping toward the sound. T. rex! Dino-Mike recognized the monstrous stomps without even looking.

Dino-Mike ran. He circled around and headed right for Mr. Bones. He was going to give him a taste of his own medicine. The T. rex was getting closer, and Mike could see that Mr. Bones was in panic mode.

Mike didn't stop running as he saw Mr. Bones trying desperately to control the T. rex.

Suddenly, the T. rex stopped. Mr. Bones looked relieved. Unfortunately for him, Dino-Mike hadn't stopped running.

WHAM! He slammed into Mr. Bones with his inflated Dino Jacket.

Chapter 8
MR. BONES'S LAIR

Mr. Bones went flying into the storage doors behind him. The metal doors buckled and broke apart. That had to hurt Mr. Bones, but Mike wasn't the least bit sorry.

Dino-Mike noticed sparks coming from his Dino Jacket. The invisibility cloak was failing.

Dino-Mike was phasing in and
out of sight. That last hit he gave Mr.
Bones must have been too much for the
cloaking technology in his jacket.

Dino-Mike decided he wouldn't need
it anymore anyway and shut it off. The
jacket stopped sparking.

"Mike! In here!" came a voice.

Dino-Mike looked inside the
containment unit he knocked Mr. Bones
into, and he could see his friends.
Shannon and Jeff were tied up and
sitting on the floor inside it.

He had found them!

Mike leaped over Mr. Bones to get to
his friends.

"Oh my gosh! Mike, I'm so happy you found us!" Shannon exclaimed. "Mr. Bones destroyed the containment stakes and the battery! He found us and destroyed our equipment. We couldn't stop him!"

"Don't worry," said Dino-Mike. "I'm here."

"Oh, I would worry a little bit if I were you," came the deep voice.

Mike looked up to see Mr. Bones rising.

"You need to realize that either now or later you will surrender," Mr. Bones said. "There is no place for you to run up here." Mr. Bones was blocking the only way out. "Now that you're cornered in here, and there's nothing but dinosaurs out there . . . give me the jacket!"

Mike reached his hand inside of his jacket to activate balloon mode but nothing happened. He tried again.

Still nothing.

"What's the matter?" whispered

Shannon.

"I don't know," Mike whispered back.

"I think my jacket short-circuited."

"What are we going to do?" asked

Jeff.

"I have an idea," said Dino-Mike.

"Just hold on to something."

Even if the Dino Jacket wasn't

working, there was one high-tech add-

on that still might function — the rocket

pack!

Dino-Mike didn't hesitate. He flipped

the rocket pack on, and he took off like,

well, a ROCKET!

FWOOOOOOOOSH!

The pack's high-pressured air sent

him flying right at Mr. Bones.

Mr. Bones tried to move out of the way, but he wasn't quick enough. Dino-Mike struck him — **SMASH!** — and knocked him down.

Mike quickly shut off the rocket and landed.

"You are a frustrating little boy!" screamed Mr. Bones, jumping to his feet again and racing at Mike.

Dino-Mike quickly turned around and ignited his rocket pack again. The high-pressured air sent Mr. Bones flying across the room.

WHAM! He smashed into the far wall.

"Come on!" Mike shouted at Jeff and Shannon, waving them to the exit.

"Mike!" cried Jeff. "You got some sick moves, bro!"

Shannon nodded, and then said, "Let's put an end to this guy right now!"

They turned to face Mr. Bones, but he was already on his feet and on top of them. He quickly locked Shannon in his arms. "Try that again," shouted Mr. Bones, "and your girlfriend's going along for the ride, too!"

"She's not my girlfriend!" Dino-Mike shot back. But Shannon was his best friend, and he needed to help her — and fast!

Chapter 9
EARTHQUAKE PILL

"Let her go!" Mike shouted, although he knew Mr. Bones would never do such a thing.

"BWAHAHAHA!" Mr. Bones laughed.

With one arm holding tight to Shannon, Mr. Bones used the other hand to command another dinosaur.

A nearby allosaurus let loose an incredible **ROOOOOOAAAAARRR!**

Jeff and Mike looked up at the beast.
The dino lunged at them, snapping its
ultrastrong jaws. Jeff and Mike knew
enough about dinosaur attacks to start
running in different directions. The jaws
of the giant beast snapped between them
as they barely got out of the way.

CRUNCH! CRUNCH!

This is useless, Mike thought as he ran. The whole situation was like a tennis match where the ball keeps going from one side of the court to the other. The fight keeps going back and forth between them. Mr. Bones would get the upper hand, and then they would. No one would blame Mike for the effort.

Something needed to give! Dino-Mike needed to save Shannon, and he needed to end this battle once and for all.

Mike knew that the key to defeating Mr. Bones was taking away his remote-control glove. They'd tried again and again but had never been able to get it.

Thoughts were swirling in his head. Then an idea struck him!

He had been thinking about this whole thing all wrong. All this time and through all those countries, Dino-Mike and his friends had been trying to steal Mr. Bones's glove away from him. Maybe they needed him to take it off himself!

Dino-Mike stopped and let the allosaurus stomp toward him.

BOOM! BOOM! BOOM! BOOM! BOOM!

Soon the allosaurus was almost directly overhead. Its large foot hovered in the air, threatening to come down on top of Dino-Mike.

"MIKE!" Shannon cried out.

"STOP!" Mike yelled just in time.

Mr. Bones held up the gloved hand that controlled the dinosaur. The allosaurus suddenly stopped, foot still hanging in the air.

"Enough," said Mike, breathing heavily. "I've had enough . . . I give up."

"Mike! No!" said Jurassic Jeff. "You can't do that! We're so close."

"There's just too many, Jeff. This . . . " Mike pointed to the very large allosaurus, " . . . was going to trample me. I mean, every time it takes a step it's like a mini EARTHQUAKE!"

Mr. Bones kept an eye on both of them, listening carefully.

"It's not worth it," Mike said, starting to unzip his Dino Jacket.

"Mike, no!" Shannon cried again.

"I'm sorry, Shannon," Mike said. "I can't be chased by dinosaurs anymore." He slipped the jacket off of his shoulders and folded it. "I can't do earthquakes anymore." Mike was sure to look at Jeff.

Jurassic Jeff was even more puzzled than before.

"Earthquakes, Jeff," Dino-Mike repeated. "No more EARTHQUAKES!"

"Ohhhhh!" Jurassic Jeff finally realized Dino-Mike's plan.

Mr. Bones went back and forth between them, weary of any tricks.

Mike kept Mr. Bones's attention on him when he took a few steps toward the masked man. With one hand held in the air to show he wasn't hiding anything, Dino-Mike held up the jacket with the other. Mr. Bones slowly reached out his gloved hand for the jacket as he continued to hold Shannon with the other hand.

"It's time you came to your senses," said Mr. Bones. "I've finally caught you!"

"I'm done with everything except one last thing," Mike added.

"And what is that?" asked Mr. Bones.

Jeff rummaged in his pocket and pulled out what looked like a small rock.

"Why don't you catch this!" he said, tossing the device at Mr. Bones.

Mr. Bones's reaction was quick as he reached out his gloved controlled hand to catch the object. "What is this?" he asked. "You tried to stop me with a rock?"

"It's not a rock." Jeff smiled.

Mr. Bones inspected the object closer. "What is it?"

"It's an earthquake pill," explained Dino-Mike. "Or in this case, a moonquake pill."

Suddenly, the earthquake device activated. Mr. Bones's hand started to shake. "What is this? What's going on?!"

Mr. Bones's hand continued to tremble. "What have you done?"

"That's what Jeff calls a seismic pellet," said Shannon. "It causes a mini earthquake."

Mr. Bones quickly opened his hand to let the pellet drop but nothing did.

"Yeah, that's not going to work," said Jeff. "It absorbed into your glove. It's pretty much going shake your whole arm until it falls off if you don't take that glove off."

Mr. Bones's hand and arm started to shake more violently. He was forced to let go of Shannon to use that hand to take off the glove. It was difficult to do as his hand was shaking so badly.

Dino-Mike smiled and put his jacket back on as he watched the comical scene play out before him. They watched as Mr. Bones tried to take off the glove.

Mr. Bones's one hand wouldn't cooperate with the other. Mr. Bones writhed and wiggled as his whole body was now shaking.

"Ahhh!" he screamed. "Stop this thing! Please!!"

After a while, Mr. Bones finally managed to get the glove off and it dropped to the ground. The glove shook so hard that it literally started to shake apart.

CRASSSHHHH!

The high-tech glove broke into tiny little fragments and then into smaller fragments and then into little pieces of dust.

"What have you done!" Mr. Bones began screaming. "You've ruined everything!"

"Relax, psycho evil guy," said Jeff. "All we did was destroy your ability to control these dinosaurs."

"YES! Exactly!" said Mr. Bones, pulling off his face mask. "And what do you expect the dinosaurs to do now that they're out of my control?!"

"Um," Mike muttered. "I guess I didn't think that far ahead."

"So you're saying, " Shannon added, "all of these dinosaurs are —"

"Free to do whatever they want?" Jeff Jurassic interrupted.

The roar of the T. rex was the next thing they heard.

Chapter 10
DINOSAUR RAMPAGE

They all scattered. Dinosaurs were running amok in all different directions. Dino-Mike managed to hide behind a large column with Shannon, but they knew that wouldn't be much of a hiding place if any one of these dinosaurs decided to come their way.

"This is crazy!" said Shannon. "All of these dinos in this small space. It won't be long before something bad happens."

Mr. Bones dove behind a large container to avoid a group of raptors. "We need to get to the teleport control room!" he shouted at the others.

"You can teleport them without your glove?" asked Jeff, still running for his life.

"Over there!" Mr. Bones pointed to the other side of the open area where there were about thirty dinosaurs between them and the room.

THOOM! Suddenly there was a loud noise behind Mike and Shannon. They turned to see the stegosaurus smashing its tail on the glass wall of the facility.

Shannon grabbed Mike by the arm.

"If that dinosaur breaks that reinforced wall we'll all get —" she began.

"Sucked out into space!" Mike finished.

"Yes," Shannon confirmed, "Even the dinosaurs."

Dino-Mike and Shannon started to make a break for the control room. Jeff and even Mr. Bones were trying to make their way there too, all weaving in between dinosaurs. Luckily, there were so many dinosaurs and they were so preoccupied with each other that all four of them were able to make it to the door.

Dino-Mike was there first and tried to get in. "It's locked!"

Shannon turned to Mr. Bones. "Do you have the key?"

"No. My glove activated the lock," said Mr. Bones. "I have no way of opening it."

Dino-Mike struggled to open it.

"It's no use," said Mr. Bones. "It's a reinforced door to keep out dinosaurs."

Dino-Mike noticed a small window on the door. "The window!"

Jurassic Jeff grabbed the skull mask Mr. Bones was still holding. He wrapped his fist with it and smashed the window in!

"What good will that do?" asked Shannon. "That window is too small for any of us to get through it!"

Dino-Mike immediately thought to use his jacket somehow. But then he quickly remembered, and said, "My jacket is completely dead!"

"Oh, great," said Shannon.

Then she turned and pointed a finger at Mr. Bones. "You realize that we wouldn't be in this mess if it wasn't for you!"

Mr. Bones lowered his head. "I'm quickly realizing that," he said.

"There's no time for blaming him right now," said Jurassic Jeff. "We need a plan — and fast!"

The T. rex loomed closer. Jeff braced himself against the door. Mike tried desperately to get something in his jacket to work. When that didn't work he looked around and spotted something. Behind the T. rex, staying close, was the baby T. rex.

Mike realized it was the momma T. rex and baby T. rex they had encountered out on the moonscape.

"I've got an idea!" said Mike. "Everyone stay here and wait for my signal. When I give it, run!"

"Mike, no!" Shannon screamed. "Your jacket's not working!"

"Yeah, but the jacket's not all that makes me Dino-Mike," Mike said. "I've still got my brain!" With that he took off running.

"Wait!" Jeff called out. "How will we know the signal? What is it?"

Mike didn't respond. *They'll know,* he thought.

Dino-Mike sprinted right at the
momma T. rex. He slid between the
creature's legs and then scooped up the
baby T. rex behind it.

ROOOOOAARRRR!!

The momma T. rex growled and then turned and followed Mike. Mike ran at full speed, hugging the kidnapped baby dinosaur closely. There were other dinosaurs running around the entire complex. It was total chaos as Mike attempted to navigate his way through them. He ran in a zigzagged pattern but then ultimately headed for the door where everyone else was waiting.

"Run!" yelled Mike.

Taking that as the signal, Jeff, Shannon, and Mr. Bones ran away from the door. Mike stuffed the little baby T. rex through the smashed-out window.

He was careful not to hurt it and to make sure the mother T. rex saw exactly what he was doing.

The angry momma T. rex snapped her jaws at Mike as he moved away from the door. Mike hid behind some containers Jeff, Shannon, and Mr. Bones had found nearby. They watched as the maternal instincts of the large animal took over.

She roared so loud that all the other dinos made sure to stay away from the area. She then proceeded to shred with her giant teeth until the door was cut to ribbons. She tore away the remains of the door and set loose her little baby.

Momma T. rex looked around for any sign of Mike. When she did not see him, she stomped away with the baby T. rex hugging close to her legs!

Chiang looked up in shock.

Shannon scolded him. "See! That's why your don't mess with dinosaurs!"

"Trust me, dude, she's right!" said Jeff. "I've learned from experience."

He then grabbed Mr. Bones's coat by the back of his neck and dragged him into the control room. "Come on," Jeff told him. "Let's transport these dinosaurs somewhere on Earth where they won't do any harm until we can get them to their proper times."

Dino-Mike and Shannon sat back behind the containers. Mike let out a long sigh of relief. Shannon punched him in the arm.

"Ow! What was that for?" asked Mike.

"For taking all those dumb chances where you could have gotten really hurt," she said.

Dino-Mike smiled because he knew that Shannon really cared about him. They both sat behind the containers and out of sight laughing, knowing their Bones Twins ordeal was finally over.

There was the sound of rushing wind and then a loud **POP**.

A large allosaurus disappeared. Moon dust was kicked up but started to settle back down. The pop sounds followed consistently as one by one the dinosaurs disappeared from the Moon.

Jurassic Jeff was taking Mr. Bones back to Earth to make sure he wouldn't run away again. Before he left, he showed Mike and Shannon how to use the transport device and set the coordinates.

"All you need to do is hit this button and stand over there and you'll be all set," said Jeff.

Mr. Bones didn't say anything. The look on his face was all anyone needed.

Shannon hit the button. With a quick rush of air and the loud pop, Jeff and Mr. Bones were gone.

As the dust settled, Mike looked at Shannon. "Well, I guess we should be going," he said.

She looked at him and said, "Well, who says we have to go back right now? We're on the Moon. Maybe we can go explore it a bit."

Dino-Mike was excited for a second and then frowned. "My jacket. It doesn't work!"

"That's because you took all those unnecessary chances," said Shannon. She punched Mike softly on the arm.

FRITZ! BANG! WHIZ! The Dino Jacket suddenly came back to life.

"Hey! You got my jacket to work!" exclaimed Mike.

They stared at each other for a few seconds. They both smiled. Then they quickly prepped themselves and ran to the air lock. Shannon hit the button to the door, and they bounced outside onto the surface of the Moon.

Mike hit the button on his jacket, and he took off like a rocket. "This is awesome!" he shouted with delight.

GLOSSARY

Jurassic Period (juh-RASS-ik PEER-ee-uhd)—a period of time about 200 to 144 million years ago

fossil (FAWSS-uhl)—the remains, impression, or trace of a living thing of a former geologic age, like a dinosaur bone

Changyuraptor Yangi (JYAHNG-yoo-RAP-tor JAN-gee)—a four-winged predatory dinosaur, also known as C. yangi

paleontologist (pale-ee-uhn-TOL-uh-jist)—a scientist who deals with fossils and other ancient life-forms

Tyrannosaurus rex (ti-RAN-uh-sor-uhss REKS)—a large, meat-eating dinosaur that walked on its hind legs, also known as a T. rex

DINO JOKES!

Q: What do you call a dinosaur that steps on a car?
A: Tyrannosaurus Wrecks.

Q: What toys do dinosaurs play with?
A: Tricera-tops.

Q: What do you call a dinosaur stuck in a glacier?
A: A fossicle.

Q: Who is the fastest dinosaur?
A: A prontosaurus.

Q: What days of the week do raptors eat their food?
A: Chewsday.

Q: Where was the T. rex when the
   sun set?
A: In the dark.

Q: Why do museums display old
   dinosaur bones?
A: They can't afford the new ones.

Q: Where does a triceratops sit?
A: On its tricera-bottom.

Q: What makes more noise than
   a dinosaur?
A: Ten dinosaurs!

Q: What do you call a dinosaur that
   talks and talks and talks?
A: A dino-bore.

ABOUT THE AUTHOR

Bronx, New York–born writer and artist Franco Aureliani has been drawing comics since he could hold a crayon. Currently residing in upstate New York with his wife, Ivette, and son, Nicolas, he spends most of his days in his Batcave-like studio where he works on comics projects. In 1995, Franco founded Blindwolf Studios, an independent art studio where he and fellow creators can create children's comics. Franco is the creator, artist, and writer of Weirdsville, L'il Creeps, and Eagle All Star, as ˮ   and writer of Patrick

Franco recently
Superman Family A
Titans by DC Comi   )oy
and Aw Yeah Comic   :s.
When he's not writ   :o
teaches high school